NO LONGER PROPERTY OF
ANYTHINK LIBRARIES/
RANGEVIEW LIBRARY DISTRICT

D0603294

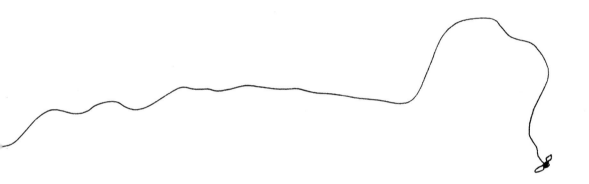

The
Flat Rabbit

Text and illustrations © 2011 Bárður Oskarsson
Translation © 2014 Marita Thomsen

Published in North America in 2014 by Owlkids Books Inc.

Published in the Faroe Islands under the title *Flata Kaninin* in 2011 by BFL, Faroe Islands, www.bfl.fo

All rights reserved. No part of this publication may be reproduced, stored in a retrieval system, or transmitted in any form or by any means, without the prior written permission of Owlkids Books Inc., or in the case of photocopying or other reprographic copying, a license from the Canadian Copyright Licensing Agency (Access Copyright). For an Access Copyright license, visit www.accesscopyright.ca or call toll-free to 1-800-893-5777.

Owlkids Books acknowledges the financial support of the Canada Council for the Arts, the Ontario Arts Council, the Government of Canada through the Canada Book Fund (CBF) and the Government of Ontario through the Ontario Media Development Corporation's Book Initiative for our publishing activities.

Published in Canada by	Published in the United States by
Owlkids Books Inc.	Owlkids Books Inc.
10 Lower Spadina Avenue	1700 Fourth Street
Toronto, ON M5V 2Z2	Berkeley, CA 94710

Library and Archives Canada Cataloguing in Publication

Oskarsson, Bárður, 1972- [Flata kaninin. English]
The flat rabbit / Bárður Oskarsson ; translated by Marita Thomsen.

Translation of: Flata kaninin. ISBN 978-1-77147-059-9 (bound)

    I. Thomsen, Marita, translator II. Title. III. Title: Flata kaninin. English.

PZ7.O825Fl 2014   j839'.6993   C2014-900394-3

Library of Congress Control Number: 2014932277

Manufactured in Dongguan, China, in March 2014, by Toppan Leefung Packaging & Printing (Dongguan) Co., Ltd.
Job #BAYDC7

A   B   C   D   E   F

Publisher of Chirp, chickaDEE and OWL
www.owlkidsbooks.com

THE FLAT RABBIT

Bárður Oskarsson

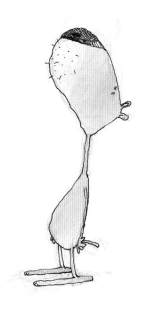

"Good grief! Would you look at her!" said the rat when she spotted the rabbit.

"Um...yes. I was just wondering what she was doing there," replied the dog, a bit startled. It had been so quiet until the rat came along.

"She is totally flat," said the rat. For a while they just stood there looking at her.

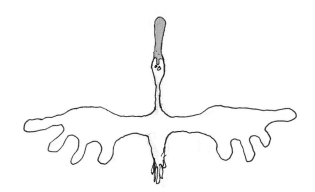

"Do you know her?"

"Well," said the dog, "I think she's from number 34. I've never talked to her, but I peed on the gate a couple of times, so we've definitely met."

The rat thought it was all a bit sad.

"Lying there can't be any fun," she said, looking at the dog.

"That was exactly what I thought when I found her," said the dog.

The rat pondered this for a while, and then she said, "Maybe we should move her?"

The dog agreed. But where would they take her?

They went to the park to think.

At least the dog was thinking—so hard that his brain was creaking.

Where could they move her? And what if somebody found her and ate her?

They could leave her outside number 34, but what would the people there think if they saw a dog and a rat bringing back their rabbit, totally flattened? No good would come of that.

The dog was now so deep in thought that, had you put your ear to his skull, you would have actually heard him racking his brain.

"That's it!" said the dog suddenly.

And after explaining his idea to the rat, they both went back for the flat rabbit.

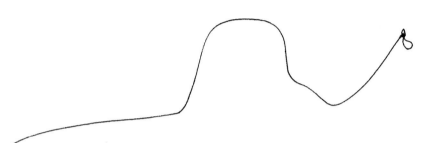

"Watch the ears!" said the dog, while carefully peeling her flat legs off the road.

The rabbit was so thin, he was afraid she might tear.

It was already evening when they reached the dog's house.

They worked all night on their plan.

You could hear them chatting and hammering away in the doghouse. Nobody knew what was going on in there.

When the job was done, the sun was already out again.

The dog was quite proud of their excellent work, but the rat wasn't convinced the tape would hold.

After the dog had assured the rat that it would, they went to the park.

It is not that easy to fly a kite. You need a bit of wind, but not too much. And you have to run extremely quickly, but not forget to keep an eye on the kite.

They raced back and forth forty-two times before they managed to get the kite in the air.

Once the kite was flying, they watched it in silence for a long time.

"Do you think she is having a good time?" the rat finally asked, without looking at the dog.

The dog tried to imagine what the world would look like from up there.

"I don't know…" he replied slowly. "I don't know."

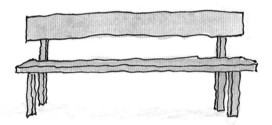

The kite was now so high up in the air they almost couldn't see the rabbit on it anymore.

And while they were watching, the dog asked, "Would you like a turn?"

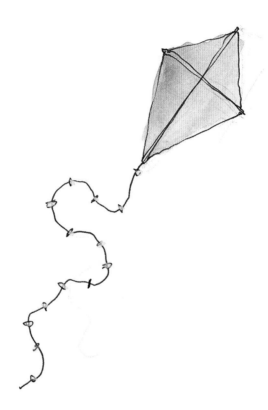

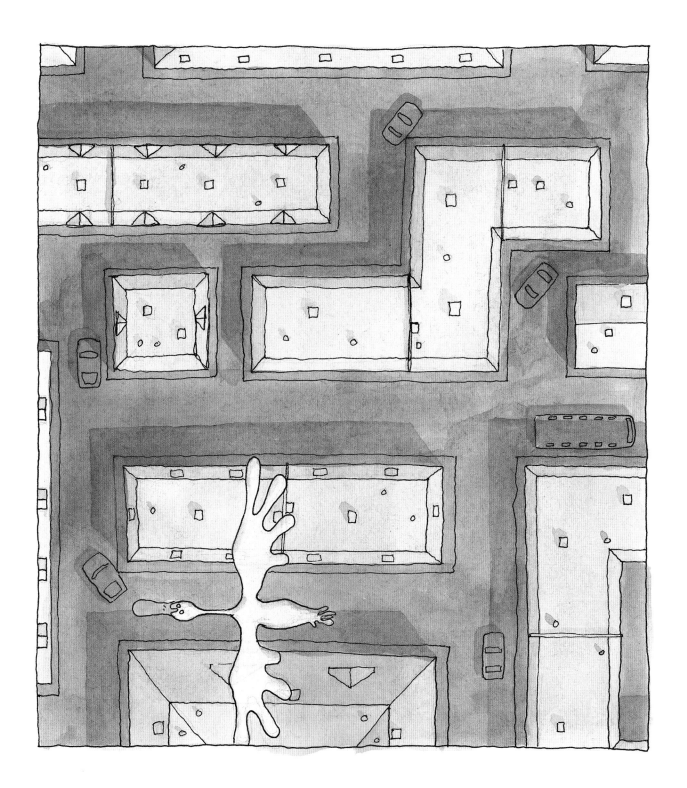